Laurina

the Enchanted being

WRITTEN AND ILLUSTRATED BY GHOST LAYNE

" This book is dedicated to all the kindhearted beings in this world.
Do not let negativity dim your light.
You have so much to offer this world, starting with your smile."

This book belongs to:

Once there was the most beautiful human like creature that ever lived.

Her name was Laurina.

Her hair was so long and luxurious like a dark chocolate river flowing down her back.

She had beautiful brown skin that was clearer than the sky on a cold winter's night.

Her eyes had the most loving sparkle that could easily be mistaken for diamonds.

But her heart was the real treasure in all her beauty.

Laurina was so loving and kind to anyone who came across her path.

She had the most power in all the land that she could mend a broken heart with just a touch of the hand.

She brought warmth to people and their lives by just being present and sharing a cup of tea with them.

Laurina was the most rare creature that ever lived.

However, just like everything else the humans started to take her for granted.

They were selfish creatures, they wanted her power for their own.

Laurina was so pure of heart and selfless that she had an invisible shield around her.

No human could touch her unless she allowed them to.

It started from one human and spread like wildfire with the anger and resentment that they showed toward Laurina.

The rage got worse within days from when the first humans wanted Laurina's power as their own.

All the humans' focus were on her gifts to be used as a weapon of power against others.

The beauty of her gifts to love unconditionally were no longer a thought, as that is where her power derived from.

Laurina tried for weeks and months and years after the start of the first envy, to show the humans how to love and be selfless again but to no avail did they listen.

Laurina's heart started to break to see all the humans she loved inside and out turn into such horrendous living things.

Surely their hearts will turn to stone if they kept up this hatred for another day, thought Laurina.

Laurina loved her humans more than she loved herself that she decided to do the only thing she could in order to stop their hearts from turning to stone.

Laurina's heart broke a bit more as she packed up a few of her things and left the town on foot to find a secluded place to live for eternity.

Laurina was made to love others and show them how to love.

If she was not able to share that gift her heart would shatter day by day until it was completely broken.

It went from days to weeks that Laurina walked, she wanted to make sure that she saved the humans hearts so she knew she had to go as far away as possible.

Just as she lost count of the days and weeks she had been walking for, she saw a bed of water in front of her.

She knew this was where she would have to live the remainder of her time until her heart was completely shattered to unfixable pieces.

Laurina set her bag of things she brought with her on a tree stump and started to weep.

She knew this was surely the end of her and the love she could give as all that was with her was nature.

She could give her love to the plants and creatures around to slow the process of her heart shattering but it was not enough as Laurina was made to love the humans.

Day by day Laurina made a daily task to do everyday to keep her mind busy.

She woke at the light of sunrise and spent time with any animals that passed through her path.

Then after an hour or so she would work to fix her a small cottage to live in as well as more things that she would need in the area.

Again, weeks and months have passed as Laurina made the cottage into a home and the woodland creatures kept her shattering heart at a slow break.

She longed to be with her humans again to love them wholeheartedly but she loved them more than she loved herself that she would not risk them turning to stone so she wept again that night.

Years have passed and the elders of the humans shared her story of a beautiful creature that used to live in town that was so powerful and loving.

As the story continued to be told over the years the more the story changed.

All that was the truth in the now told "legend of the beautiful creature" was that she was a beauty like no other and that she just disappeared from the town and the town grew with rage and hate since she left.

This was the year that a baby girl was born that was pure of heart, her name was Katya.

She grew up hearing the story of the beautiful creature that unconditionally loved humans and brought warmth to everyone's hearts.

Katya had so much sorrow in her heart that she was brought into a world with such hate and sadness.

Katya would search everyday for more information on the legend of the beautiful creature.

She needed to learn all she could about what the creature was and what she could do.

More importantly she wanted to know why she abandoned the humans if the creature was meant to love them.

As Katya reached her thirteenth birthday she prepared for the day she would embark on the journey to find this legend.

The day had finally come for Katya's birth celebration; she promised her parents she would stay until the end of her party.

As promised, Katya waited until the last song to play that ended the party and she kissed her parents goodbye.

Katya left as swift as the midnight wind into the woods to start her journey.

Days and weeks have passed and Katya moved from town to town passing through each one within a few days.

Her focus was like a hawk to get to the beautiful legend in hopes to restore what was left of humanity.

As time passed Katya started to notice that she never felt the need to rest or had any pains of hunger or thirst.

Kayta was confused but she just pushed it to the back of her mind and kept moving on pace.

Several months passed and she finally saw a small little cottage near a bank of water.

Katya was certain that she had reached her destination. Only to her surprise Laurina was waiting for her.

Laurina slowly walked out of the cottage to greet Katya.

Young Katya had so many emotions going through her body as she finally met the most beautiful legend that she grew up learning about.

The young girl was stunned by such beauty that one creature could hold.

As soon as Laurina reached out her hand to Katya, the young girl collapsed into a deep slumber.

Laurina prepared the house for when Katya would wake.

Laurina wanted everything perfect for the young girl to be comfortable and have all she could eat.

Thus, for the young girl would regain her strength for her journey home.

Katya slept for three days and two nights.

On the third night Katya woke well rested and famished.

Laurina already had the fire going and the table set from end to end with different foods.

Katya and Laurina spent the night talking about Katya's travels and enjoying all the food Laurina had made for her.

With every bite that Katya took the stronger she felt.

Katya was confused as she did not hunger for food or water the entire trip that was months long.

The last time Katya could remember eating at all was at her birth celebration.

Katya shared her confusion with Laurina.

Laurina slightly smiled and said she knew Katya was coming to find her.

Laurina told the young girl how she granted the girls' food and water the lasting longevity.

So this way Katya could make it to her without having to worry of food or water as well as her sleep.

Katya was lost in amazement with how thoughtful and loving Laurina was.

How much she did for a child she did not know, who didn't even know her name.

Laruina then told Katya what her purpose was in the human realm and the true events that caused Laurina to leave the humans.

This is when Katya also learned of Laurina's slow shattering heart with help from the woodland creatures that helped slow the breaking process.

The young girl grasped for Laurina and fell into tears.

Katya knew she would have to do all she could to love Laurina's heart back together.

The young girl knew it was up to her to make Laurina's heart strong enough to make it back to the humans so Laurina could be whole again.

It has been a month since Katya made her first step onto Laurina's cottage.

Laurina's heart was almost halfway mended and life was brought back into her face.

Katya knew it was time to go and restore Laurina to the town she once left.

Laurina decided that they would leave that Sunday.

Katya and Laurina spent the rest of the days they had left organizing and packing what Laurina wanted to take.

As the day for departure came closer the woodland creatures came one by one to bid farewell.

On the final day Laurina blessed her cottage goodbye. It was bitter sweet as this was where she made and found refuge for over a decade.

With this final goodbye the cottage was able to lay to rest.

Every tree, moss and dirt was able to go back to the earth from where they came from as before.

Laurina and Katya started walking back toward the town that Laurina had fled from.

Now that her heart was mended more than before she was able to cast a sleep over the human realm and all that walked it.

Once the sleep was casted, Laurina grabbed Katya and replanted herself and the young girl to the town.

Laurina broke the sleep of the human realm the morning after her and the young girl were back in the town.

When Katya woke she did not probe Laurina of how she was back in her town as she knew this magnificent creature was only capable of good.

Katya conveyed to Laurina that she was going to let her parents know she has returned and with a huge gift to the land.

The beautiful being nodded in understanding and acknowledged that she will prepare herself to be presented to the humans.

Katya's parents embraced the young girl at the immediate sight of her return.

Katya spoke to her parents all about her travels and all the wonderful things that she was able to witness at the hand of Laurina.

The father told Katya that they should have a celebration to welcome the legend back to the town.

The parents confessed to Katya how much she was deeply missed from the land.

How delighted that the humans would be that she chose to come back home in their lifetime.

Word spread without delay of the enchanted being's return to the land.

The humans were over joyed of her return and all the love she would restore to mankind and their hearts.

Katya's parents informed all the humans in town of the celebration that would take place to welcome Laurina back.

In hopes to show her their appreciation for her decision to bless the humans with her return home.

Katya went back to Laurina to help her get ready for the celebration that was to take place in a few hours.

Laurina's heart was almost completely mended at this point, her long dark chocolate hair looked like a flowing river in the sunset once again.

Laurina and Katya arrived at the celebration hand in hand.

As much as the humans and Katya needed Laurina, Laurina needed Katya for reassurance and the humans for her heart to be whole.

The humans were astonished at the sight of the enchanted being and began to weep.

How could humans cause such a wonderful being to leave?

At this point they knew humans were the cause of this legend's departure.

The humans knew that for whatever reason it was they were the ones that took this beautiful creature for granted.

Laurina sensed this feeling amongst the humans in the land and the last broken pieces in her heart were whole.

As now she could stay and love the humans once again as she was originally designed for.

The humans made a pledge to tell the original story that once happened to the enchanted being that caused her to leave.

Thus, mankind would never get blindsided and take Laurina's gifts and unconditional love for granted again.

THE END

Made in the USA
Columbia, SC
27 December 2021

52865340R00020